HEIDI HECKELBECK

Might Be Afraid of the Dark

By Wanda Coven
Illustrated by Priscilla Burris

LITTLE SIMON

New York London Toronto Sydney New Delhi

LITTLE SIMON
An imprint of Simon & Schuster Children's Publishing Division
1230 Avenue of the Americas, New York, New York 10020
First Little Simon paperback edition October 2015
Copyright © 2015 by Simon & Schuster, Inc.
Also available in a Little Simon hardcover edition.
All rights reserved, including the right of reproduction in whole or in part in any form. LITTLE SIMON is a registered trademark of Simon & Schuster, Inc., and associated colophon is a trademark of Simon & Schuster, Inc. For information about special discounts for bulk purchases, please contact Simon & Schuster Special Sales at 1-866-506-1949 or business@simonandschuster.com. The Simon & Schuster Speakers Bureau can bring authors to your live event. For more information or to book an event contact the Simon & Schuster Speakers Bureau at 1-866-248-3049 or visit our website at www.simonspeakers.com.
Designed by Ciara Gay
Manufactured in the United States of America 0915 FFG
10 9 8 7 6 5 4 3 2 1
Library of Congress Cataloging-in-Publication Data
Coven, Wanda.
Heidi Heckelbeck might be afraid of the dark / by Wanda Coven ; illustrated by Priscilla Burris. — First edition.
pages cm. — (Heidi Heckelbeck ; 15)
Summary: Going to her first sleepover, Heidi tries to hide her fear of the dark, with a little help from her *Book of Spells*.
ISBN 978-1-4814-4627-3 (pbk : alk. paper) —
ISBN 978-1-4814-4628-0 (hc : alk. paper) — ISBN 978-1-4814-4629-7 (eBook)
[1. Fear of the dark—Fiction. 2. Sleepovers—Fiction. 3. Witches—Fiction.]
I. Burris, Priscilla, illustrator. II. Title.
PZ7.C83393Hl 2015
[Fic]—dc23
2014044015

CONTENTS

SCAREDY-CAT

Click!

Click!

Click!

Heidi switched on three lights: The bedroom light, the bathroom light, and the hall light. Then she kicked off her slippers and hopped into bed.

"I'm ready!" she called.

She listened to her mother's foot-steps as they came down the hall and into her room.

Her mom sighed. "It looks like day-time when you go to bed. Let me turn off *one* of these lights."

Heidi shook her head firmly.

She always slept with three lights on. She also had two flashlights stashed in her nightstand—just in case the power went out.

"Nighttime is FRIGHT time!" she

declared. Then she hid under the covers.

Her mother frowned and shook her head. "Someday you'll think being afraid of the dark is silly," she said.

Heidi pulled the covers back down and put a finger on her lips. "Shhhh!" she shushed. "I don't want Henry to hear!"

"HEAR WHAT?" shouted Henry from across the hall. "That you're SCARED of the DARK?"

"AM NOT!" Heidi shouted back. "I just like to sleep with the lights on—that's all."

Heidi heard Dad shut Henry's door. Then Dad came into Heidi's room and sat down on the bed beside Mom.

"I was afraid of the dark when I was your age too," her father said. "It means you have a very good imagination."

Heidi sat up in bed. "It does?"

Dad nodded.

"Well, that's a relief!" Heidi said, falling back on her pillow. She was happy to know there was *something* good about being afraid of the dark. Her parents looked at each other.

"But you still have to get your imagination under control," her father added.

"Oh," said Heidi. "Merg."

Chapter 2

GiRLS ONLY!

Heidi spied a pink envelope in her cubby at school the next day. It had her name on it in swirly letters. *What's this?* she thought excitedly as she snatched the envelope.

"Go ahead, open it!" said Heidi's best friend, Lucy Lancaster.

Lucy had the cubby next to Heidi's.

The girls walked into the hallway to get away from the end-of-the-day cubbyhole rush.

Then Heidi slipped her finger under the cupcake seal and pulled out a pillowcase-shaped card. Across the top in pink polka-dot letters it read *SLUMBER PARTY!*

Underneath that it said *Come celebrate Lucy's birthday!*

"You're having a slumber party!" exclaimed Heidi.

Lucy nodded. "Yup, this Saturday!" she said.

"Who's coming?" asked Heidi.

Lucy's smile faded. "Well," she began, "I was only going to invite a few people, but my mom made me invite EVERYONE."

"The entire class?" questioned Heidi.

"No, silly! Just the *girls*!"

Heidi hit her forehead with the palm of her hand. "Please don't tell me Melanie's invited!"

Melanie Maplethorpe was Heidi's least favorite girl in the class.

Lucy sighed. "I'm sorry, but I had to include her."

Heidi crossed both her fingers and looked at the ceiling. "Please don't let her be able to make it!"

"Shh—be quiet!" whispered Lucy. "Here she comes NOW!"

Melanie skipped toward Heidi and Lucy, waving her invitation in the air.

"Hi, Lucy!" she cried. "I can't WAIT to come to your slumber party!"

Lucy forced a smile. "So glad you can make it," she said.

Then Melanie glanced at Heidi. "Is SHE coming?"

Heidi frowned.

"Of course she's coming!" said Lucy. "Heidi is my BEST friend!"

Melanie rolled her eyes. "Okay, whatever you say!" she said. "But we can still have fun—you know why?"

Lucy folded her arms. "Why?"

"Because I know some really fun games we can play!"

Heidi noticed that Lucy's face brightened at the mention of games.

"Really?" asked Lucy. "What kind of games?"

"We can play Freeze Dance!" Melanie said. "And sing karaoke songs!"

Heidi began to tap her foot on the floor. *Smell-a-nie is trying to take over Lucy's party!* she thought. *And* the weird thing is, Lucy seems to like Melanie's ideas!

"And we can have pillow fights!" added Lucy.

"And play Ghost in the Graveyard!" said Melanie.

Heidi blinked.

Ghost in the Graveyard? The name sent a shiver down her back. *That means we'll have to turn out the lights! And play in the DARK!*

Then she gulped.

And that means we'll probably have to SLEEP in the dark too!

Chapter 3

ONE LIGHT

"Mom, can we go for a walk?" asked Heidi.

Heidi and Mom went on neighbor-hood walks when Heidi needed to talk to her mom privately.

Mom looked at her watch. "I think we can squeeze in a loop before

Henry gets home from his playdate," she said.

They walked out the back door and down the driveway.

"So, pumpkin, what's on your mind?" asked Mom.

"It's about Lucy's slumber party," Heidi said. "I'm afraid to sleep in the dark."

Mom patted Heidi on the shoulder. "Would you like me to call Lucy's mother?" asked Mom. "I'm sure she would be happy to leave a light on for you."

Heidi thought about it for a

moment and then shook her head.

"But why?" asked Mom.

"Because what if Mrs. Lancaster says something in front of the other girls like 'We need to keep the lights on for *Heidi*'?"

"I doubt she would do that," said Mom.

"But what if she DID?" asked Heidi. "Do you know what would happen?"

Mom shrugged. "I can't imagine," she said.

"It means Smell-a-nie would TORTURE me for the rest of my LIFE!" said Heidi.

Mom sighed. "Then let's forget *that* idea," she said.

Heidi kicked a pebble off the curb.

"What if I picked you up before bedtime?" Mom suggested.

Heidi shook her head even harder. "Then I'd look like a BIG baby."

"And I suppose that wouldn't be good either," Mom said.

"It would be awful on a waffle!"

They walked along quietly. Mom
looked at the neighbors' gardens, and
Heidi tried not to step on the cracks
in the sidewalk.

"I have an idea," said Mom.

"What?" asked Heidi hopefully.

"Why don't you turn off one

light at bedtime
tonight?" Mom
suggested. "If you
turn out one light
every night until
the party, you'll
be ready to sleep
in the dark!"

Heidi slumped her shoulders. "What's the point?" she said. "I'll never make it to NO lights by Saturday."

"Well, you have to start somewhere," said Mom.

★ ✦ ✳ ◎ ✦

At bedtime Heidi turned on all three lights as usual.

"Don't forget our idea," Mom reminded her.

Heidi groaned and flopped onto

her bed. "I don't want to turn out a light!" she said into her pillow.

But then she pictured Melanie chanting, "Heidi is a scaredy-cat! Heidi is a scaredy-cat!" And that made Heidi sit up.

"Okay," she said in a very small voice. "One light."

"Which one?" asked Mom.

"The bathroom light," Heidi said.

Mom switched off the bathroom light. "It still looks like daytime in here," she said as she kissed Heidi good night.

"Not to me," said Heidi to herself after her mom left the room. Then she arranged her stuffed animals—a bear, a pig, a mouse, a kangaroo, and a moray eel—on either

side of her for protection. She had to lie as straight as a pretzel rod so as not to disturb her stuffed animals.

"I still don't like it," Heidi said. And then she fell fast asleep.

Everybody at Brewster Elementary bought hot lunch on Taco Tuesdays— even Melanie, who was the pickiest eater in the whole school. Melanie plopped her tray of tacos on the table and sat down next to Lucy and Heidi.

"SO!" she began. "Have you picked

out your pajamas for the slumber party yet?"

Melanie seemed to love to talk about Lucy's slumber party all the time—and Lucy seemed to like it too.

"I have!" Lucy said excitedly. "I'm wearing my pink polka-dot pajamas—just like the polka dots on my invitation. What about you?"

"I'm wearing purple gingham

check with lace around the wrists and ankles. I got them at Miss Harriet's."

Miss Harriet's Dress Shop had the most beautiful and most expensive girls' clothing in town.

"Sounds cute!" said Lucy, taking a bite of her taco.

Sounds D-U-M-B, Heidi thought.

"What kind of weirdo pajamas is SHE wearing?" whispered Melanie, pointing at Heidi.

Lucy frowned. "That's not very nice, Melanie," she said. "You need to call Heidi by her name."

"Okay, what about you, Hi-DEE?" she said.

"I'm wearing my kitten pajamas," Heidi answered.

"Oh, how cute," said Melanie. "I used to have a pair like that—in KINDERGARTEN."

Heidi crunched a taco in her hands.

"Um, let's talk more about games," said Lucy, changing the subject. "What do you think about a Suitcase Relay?"

"I love it!" said Melanie. "I thought of something fun too."

"What?" asked Lucy excitedly.

"We should tell scary stories!"

Lucy clapped her hands. "The scarier the better!" she said.

Then they both moaned like ghosts and broke into giggles.

Lucy noticed that Heidi wasn't laughing. "What's the matter?" she asked Heidi.

"Oh, nothing," Heidi said. "My tacos are a little soggy."

The truth was, Heidi had lost her appetite. She got up and cleared her tray.

Why did Melanie have to suggest scary stories? thought Heidi as she scraped her tacos into the trash. *It seems like Lucy's entire party is going to take place in the DARK.*

Then Heidi smiled. "And there's only one way to fight darkness! With LIGHT! And a little bit of magic. . . ."

Heidi was so excited that she almost hugged her dirty tray.

43

Chapter 5

NiGHT- LiGHT

Heidi dropped her books by the back door and ran upstairs to her bedroom. Then she pulled her *Book of Spells* out from under the bed, along with her Witches of Westwick medallion. *There has to be a spell that will make the lights stay on at Lucy's slumber party,* she thought. *If the lights are on, I won't be afraid of the dark!*

Heidi opened her book and looked through the Contents. She found a chapter called Let There Be Light! In it were spells for all kinds of lights: headlights, spotlights, warning lights, Christmas lights, and strobe lights. Then she spotted one that looked just right: night-lights.

"That's it!" exclaimed Heidi.

She flipped to the page and read over the spell.

The Night-Light Spell

Has the power ever gone out at your house? Perhaps you have a pesky lamp that won't stay on? Or are you the kind of witch who's simply AFRAID OF THE DARK? Then this is the spell for YOU!

Ingredients:

1 flashlight

1 half-peeled orange

2 birthday candles

1 plastic zipper storage bag

Place the flashlight and the birthday candles in the plastic storage bag and seal it. Lay your Witches of Westwick medallion on top of the plastic bag and put your left hand over it. Hold the half-peeled orange in your right hand and whisper the following spell.

NiGHT-LiGHT! NiGHT BRiGHT! TURN THiS DARKNESS iNTO LIGHT!

This should do the trick! Heidi thought. *Now I need to find the ingredients.* She took one of the flashlights from her nightstand drawer and left it on the bed. Then she hurried downstairs. Mom and Henry were in the kitchen. When Henry saw Heidi, he waved his magic wand.

"Ta-da!" he exclaimed. "I have just made Heidi magically appear!"

Mom laughed. "Well, so you did!"

"Bravo, Houdini," said Heidi in a not-so-magical voice.

Henry waggled his eyebrows up and down. "Why, thank you," he said.

Heidi opened the refrigerator and helped herself to an orange. Then she looked around for something to eat.

"Do we have any granola bars?" she asked.

"There, in the pantry," Mom said.

Heidi scooted to the pantry and grabbed a granola bar. She also slipped two birthday candles into the front pocket of her skirt. Then

she folded a plastic storage bag and smooshed it into her back pocket.

"I'm going back upstairs to finish my homework," Heidi said.

"Sounds good," answered Mom.

Mom didn't suspect a thing.

53

Chapter 6

I GOT THIS!

Heidi leaped out of bed on Saturday morning. *Today is Lucy's slumber party!* she said to herself. She ran to her closet and pulled down her daisy overnight bag. First she packed her spell ingredients and Witches of Westwick medallion at the bottom of

the bag. Then she packed a change of clothes; her toothbrush; a hairbrush; a pillow; her stuffed bear, Bearsy; and her kitten pajamas. On second thought, she switched her kitten pajamas for her polka-dot pajamas.

Then she dashed to the hall closet and yanked her sleeping bag off the shelf. Finally, she changed and lugged everything downstairs to the kitchen.

"I'm all ready for the slumber party!" she announced.

Dad, who was sitting at the table with Henry, looked at his watch.

"It's a good thing you're ready," he said with a wink. "There's only eight hours till party time."

"I like to be prepared," said Heidi.

"Well, we still have to wrap the present," Mom said as she flipped pancakes on the griddle. When Henry heard the word "present," he looked up from his pancake.

"What did you get for Lucy?"
asked Henry. "Did you get her STINK
BOMBS?"

Heidi rolled her eyes. "Why would I
get Lucy STINK BOMBS for her birthday?" she asked.

"Because they're STINKY!" said
Henry.

Heidi let out a long huff. "Is that all boys think about?" she asked.

"Pretty much," said Henry.

"Then I promise to get you a SKUNK for your next birthday," said Heidi.

"Really?" said Henry. "You'd do that for ME?"

"Yes, she probably *would*," said Dad, giving Heidi a look. "But we have a new rule: no skunks in the house!"

"Rats," said Henry.

"No rats, either!" said Mom.

"That's not what I meant!" said Henry.

"I know," said Mom, laughing.

"Doesn't anyone care what I got for Lucy?" asked Heidi.

"Sure, we do!" said Dad. "What did you get?"

"I got her a friendship bracelet kit," said Heidi.

"EW!" said Henry.

"Fun!" said Dad.

"Would you like to wrap it your-self?" asked Mom.

"YES!" said Heidi.

"Everything's on my desk," Mom said.

Heidi zoomed to Mom's office. First she signed the fancy birthday card.

Then she wrapped the present in bumblebee wrapping paper. She had a little trouble with the ribbon.

"MOM!" called Heidi. "I need HELP!"

Mom came into the office and tied the ribbon around the present. "There!" she said. "It looks BEE-autiful!"

Heidi smiled.

"So, how are you feeling about spending the night at Lucy's?" Mom asked.

"Pretty good," said Heidi.

"Well, if you change your mind at bedtime, we can always come pick you up."

Heidi smiled to herself as she thought about her night-light spell.

"Don't worry, Mom. I GOT this," she said.

GAME ON!

Only five girls were able to make it to Lucy's slumber party: Eve Etsy; Natalie Newman; Laurel Lambert, a new girl in the class; Melanie; and Heidi. Lucy wanted to play a game called Spiderweb first. In the family room, her parents had made a gigantic spiderweb out of five strands of kitchen string. They gave everyone a clothespin. Each girl had to pick one string and wind it around the clothespin until all the strings were collected and the spiderweb was gone.

"Ready?" shouted Mrs. Lancaster. Then she blew a whistle that hung from a cord around her neck.

The girls crisscrossed the room, in and out of the web of strings.

"I wonder where my string is going to end up!" said Heidi as she bumped into Lucy.

"Me too!" said Lucy, winding her string as fast as she could.

"Is there something at the end of

the string?" asked Laurel.

"You'll see!" said Lucy.

The girls wound and wound. Finally Melanie found a goody bag at the end of her string.

"Look!" she cried. "I got a charm bracelet!"

"Me too!" exclaimed Eve. "And a ring pop!"

Everyone had a goody bag by the end of the game. The girls put on their bracelets and showed one another their charms.

The next game was the Suitcase Relay.

It was Lucy, Heidi, and Laurel against Melanie, Natalie, and Eve. Mrs. Lancaster blew the whistle. Heidi

and Natalie each raced to her team's suitcase and put on all the clothes inside, including a hat, shoes, and a necklace! Then they each posed for a picture, undressed, and ran to the back of the line.

Melanie and Lucy went last. The girls cheered for their teammates.

Then Melanie had trouble undoing her dress.

"I'm STUCK!" she cried.

She wriggled and jiggled, but she could not get free. Lucy's team won!

Then after the games, the girls sat at the dining

room table and had pizza, fruit salad, and chocolate cake with marsh-mallow frosting.

"Time to open presents, Lucy!" said Mrs. Lancaster, stacking the presents beside Lucy.

Lucy opened her gifts, thanking her friends for each one. She got a scrapbook kit from Laurel, sweet-smelling bubble bath from Eve, polka-dot slippers from Melanie, the friendship bracelet kit from Heidi, and a slumber-party box of questions from Natalie.

"Hey, let's ask each other

questions!" cried Lucy.

The girls ran to the family room and sat in a circle. Lucy read the directions.

"'Ask the girl on your left a question,'" read Lucy. "'That girl gets to answer the question AND ask the next question.' Get it?"

The girls nodded.

"Okay, I'll go first," said Lucy, turning to Natalie, the girl on her left.

"Natalie, if you could shop in any of our closets, whose would you choose?"

Natalie looked at each girl in the circle. "I'd choose Melanie's," she said.

"She has the nicest clothes of any girl in our whole school."

Melanie smiled proudly. "Thank you, Natalie!" she said sweetly.

Heidi coughed to let everyone know how SHE felt about THAT answer. Heidi and Melanie had very different styles.

"My turn!" said Natalie. She turned to Eve. "Eve, if you were a superhero, who would you be? And what super-power would you have?"

Eve rested her chin in her hand and looked up at the ceiling. "I love animals, so I would have to be Pet Girl," she said. "And my superpower would be to save all animals from harm."

"*Awwww,*" said all the girls at the same time.

Then Eve picked a card and turned

to Melanie. "Using one word, how would you describe the girl next to you?"

The girl next to Melanie happened to be Heidi.

"WEIRD!" declared Melanie.

Some of the girls giggled, but Lucy stood up for Heidi. "Okay, girls!" she cried. "Let's GET HER!"

Then Lucy playfully ran across the circle and messed up Melanie's hair. The other girls joined in, and soon everyone was laughing.

"Okay, okay!" begged Melanie, whose hair was in tangles. "I was only JOKING!"

Lucy's mom then came in and blew her whistle.

"Time to get ready for bed!" she said. "Sleeping bags and pillows to the basement!"

Heidi froze.

THE BASEMENT! she thought. *That's the darkest place in the WHOLE house! Oh no! What if my spell doesn't work down there?*

Chapter 8

THE BOY

The girls changed into their pajamas. Then they arranged their sleeping bags in a circle so each bag stuck out like a petal on a flower. They put their pillows in the middle so they could talk.

"We didn't have time to play half of

the games we thought up!" said Lucy.

"That's okay!" said Melanie. "We still have time to tell SCARY stories!"

"Oooooh!" chorused the girls.

Heidi's heart began to beat faster.

"So, who has a scary story to tell?" asked Eve.

The girls looked around the circle.
"I DO!" said Melanie.

Heidi put her hand on her spell ingredients and medallion. She had hidden them in her sleeping bag when no one was looking. But so far nobody had thought to turn out the lights.

"Okay, let's hear it!" Lucy said.

Melanie got out of her sleeping bag

and sat cross-legged on her pillow. Then her eyes grew very wide.

"This is a TRUE story," she began.

The girls squealed and poked one another.

"Once upon a time, there was a very STRANGE boy. And this very strange boy lived on Blossom Hill Road."

"Hey, that's MY street!" Lucy cried.

"It IS?" said Melanie as if she didn't know.

Lucy nodded.

"And how old was he?" asked Natalie.

"He was ten years old," said Melanie. "But he was very DIFFERENT from most ten-year-old boys. For one thing, he didn't live in a house."

"Where'd he live?" Eve asked.

"In the WOODS," said Melanie.

Heidi pulled her sleeping bag up to her neck.

"But we have WOODS right behind OUR house!" Lucy exclaimed.

Melanie nodded.

"And that's exactly where he lived,"
she said. "In YOUR woods."

The girls squealed and slid deep
into their sleeping bags.

"And there was one thing this boy always did," Melanie continued.

"What did he do?" asked Natalie.

"He whistled," said Melanie, "like this. . . ." And she began to whistle an eerie tune.

"STOP!" said Laurel. "That's SO creepy!"

Melanie stopped whistling and went on with the story. "And the boy was also known to do very strange things," she said.

"Like what?" asked Eve.

Melanie stood up, and she said, "He would always tap on windows when it was dark out. And he'd rattle the doors."

Lucy looked behind her. "Shh!" she said nervously. "I think I hear something!"

Everyone stopped to listen, but the basement was quiet.

Melanie continued the story. "The

only time anyone ever saw the boy was on rainy nights and . . ."

Cre-e-eak! The door at the top of the stairs opened.

The girls froze.

"Okay, Lucy!" called Mrs. Lancaster from the top of the stairs. "It's time for LIGHTS OUT!"

Chapter 9

RAiNDROPS

Eeeek!

Aaaah!

Ow-ee!

The girls all screamed and squirmed around in their sleeping bags at the sound of Mrs. Lancaster's voice. But not Heidi. She knew the lights were about to go off any minute, and she had to be ready to cast her spell. She carefully placed her left hand over her medallion and the plastic bag. Then she took the half-peeled orange in her right hand while she waited for the lights to go out.

"Okay, Mom," said Lucy. She turned to face her friends. "That story was SO scary!" Lucy said.

"And when the door creaked, that made it even spookier!" Eve added.

Melanie grinned triumphantly. "And it's all TRUE," she reminded them.

"And it happened in MY neighborhood," Lucy said. "I wonder why my mom never told me this story."

Melanie rested her hand on Lucy's arm. "She probably didn't want you to be afraid, that's all."

"Probably," agreed Lucy as she got up to turn off the lights.

Heidi watched Lucy reach for the light switch. *Click!* The lights went out. Heidi began to whisper the spell. Her medallion clanked against her flashlight and made a funny sound.

"What was THAT?" asked Natalie.

Heidi froze mid-spell.

"I'm not sure," Lucy answered. "It sounded like RATTLING. . . ."

Heidi quickly continued her secret night-light spell. She was so nervous about the dark that she squeezed the orange a little too hard. Suddenly the orange burst, and the juice spurted EVERYWHERE!

"Hey, did anyone just feel RAIN-DROPS?" asked Melanie in a shaky voice. She sounded really scared.

"I DID!" cried Eve.

"Me too!" said Laurel.

"Oh NO!" shouted Lucy. "It's the BOY!"

The girls screamed and began to jump this way and that. They bonked into one another in the dark and screamed even more. Heidi got

stepped on and kicked as she tried
to hide her spell ingredients.

Then Lucy's mother turned on the
lights and ran down the stairs.

"Girls!" she cried. "What in the
world is going on?"

The girls flopped onto their sleeping bags and tried to catch their breath.

"You all look as if you'd seen a *ghost*!" said Lucy's mom.

"We DID!" cried Lucy.

"Not a ghost—it was A BOY!" said Laurel, hugging her pillow.

Mrs. Lancaster shook her head and raised her eyebrows.

"A boy?" she questioned.

"Well, not a REAL boy," said Lucy. "It's just that Melanie told us a REALLY scary story. That's all."

Lucy's mom put her hands on her hips. "No more scary stories," she said firmly. "It's time to settle down."

The girls laid out their sleeping bags all over again. Then Melanie got up and whispered something in Mrs. Lancaster's ear.

Lucy's mom nodded.

"Would anyone like to leave a light on tonight?" she asked.

"Yes!" they all said at the same time.

So Lucy's mom turned on a small lamp in the corner of the room. Then she started up the stairs.

"Sweet dreams," she said. "And remember, no more scary stories!"

LET THERE BE MORE LIGHT!

Heidi snuggled into her sleeping bag. It smelled like oranges, and she could feel sticky spots here and there. She pushed the plastic bag, the mushed orange, and her medallion to the bottom of her bag with her foot.

She tried to settle down. A light was

113

on in the room, but it still wasn't as much light as she liked. She wished she could ask to have another light on, but she didn't want anyone to know she was afraid of the dark. *Let's face it,* she thought miserably. *I'm never going to get sleepy.*

Then Lucy tapped Heidi on the
elbow.

Heidi jumped, and scrunched
deeper into her sleeping bag.

"Are you awake?" she heard Lucy
whisper.

"Oh," said Heidi when she realized
it was just Lucy. "Yeah, why?"

"Because I'm really scared," said
Lucy.

Heidi rolled over. "You are?"

Lucy nodded.

"I'm scared too," Melanie said.

"Me too," said Eve.

"Same here," said Laurel.

Lucy sat up and folded her arms.
"Okay, that settles it," she said. "Let's
sleep with ALL the lights on."

The girls agreed that this was a very good idea.

Lucy got up and turned on the overhead light. The room became bright, like the middle of the day—just the way Heidi liked it! Then the girls stayed up and whispered for hours. But not Heidi.

She fell asleep just like that!

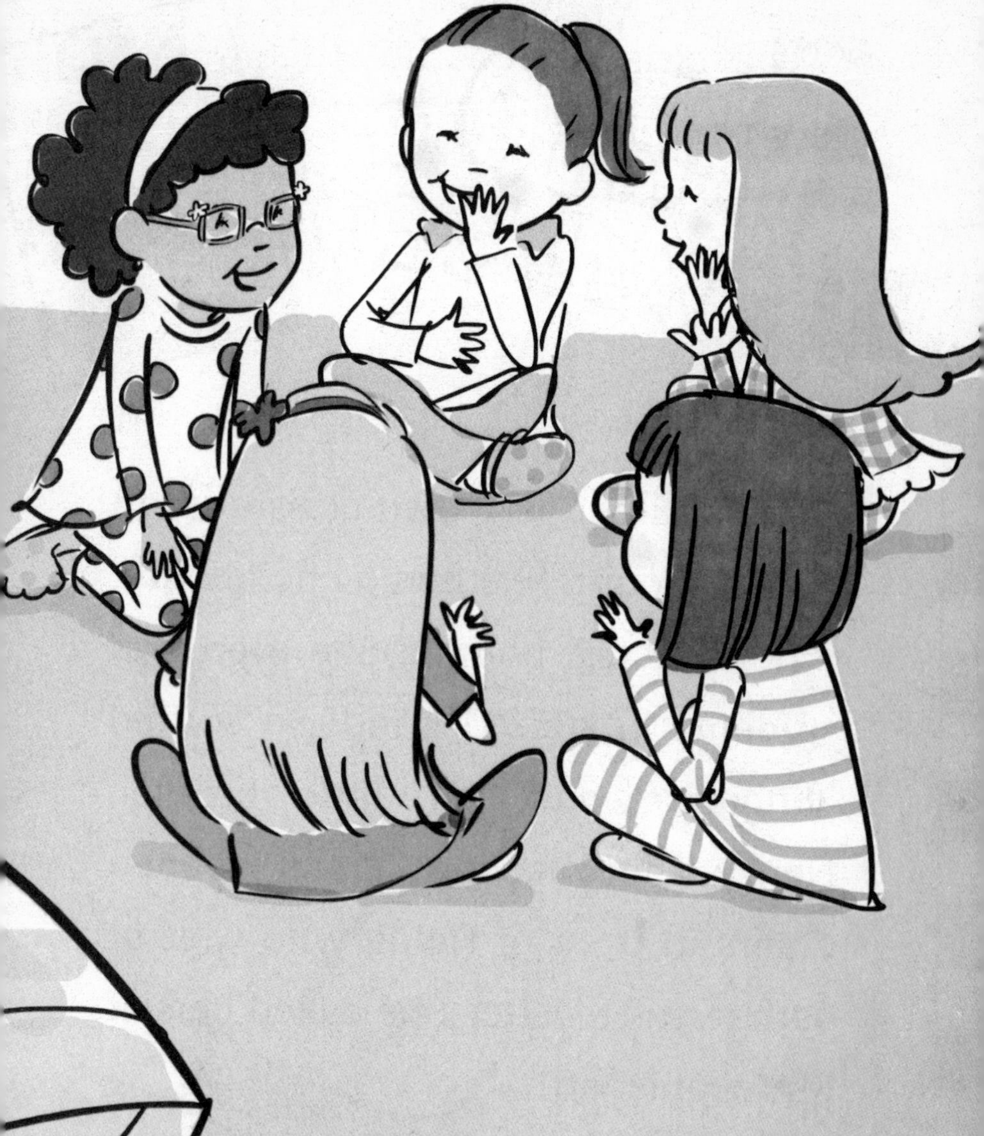

Check out the next book starring

HEIDI HECKELBECK

HEIDI HECKELBEC
Is the Bestest Babysitter!

Heidi had her very own classroom in the playroom. She had a chalkboard, a desk, and a pointer. She even had students: a stuffed panda, a stuffed kangaroo, and her little brother, Henry. They all sat on small wooden chairs in front of Heidi, who was, of course, the teacher. She called herself Mrs. Applegarth.

An excerpt from *Heidi Heckelbeck Is the Bestest Babysitter!*

Mrs. Applegarth tapped the chalk-board with her pointer. "Class, what do animals do when they're scared?"

Henry raised his hand. Mrs. Applegarth called on him.

"Skunks spray stink bombs when they're scared," he answered. "And octopuses squirt black ink."

"Very good, Henry," said Mrs. Applegarth. "You get a gold star!"

Heidi handed Henry a gold star sticker.

"Excuse me, Mrs. Applegarth!" said someone from the door.

Heidi pulled off her pretend glasses

An excerpt from *Heidi Heckelbeck Is the Bestest Babysitter!*

and looked at the door. It was Mom.

"May I help you, Mrs. Heckelbeck?"

Mom entered the classroom. She had a fancy card in her hand with gold cursive writing on it. Heidi noticed it right away.

"Ooh, what's that?" she asked, forgetting her role as make-believe teacher.

"It's a wedding invitation," Mom said.

"Do we get to go?" Heidi asked.

"It's for grown-ups this time," Mom said. "We'll need to get a babysitter."

An excerpt from *Heidi Heckelbeck Is the Bestest Babysitter!*